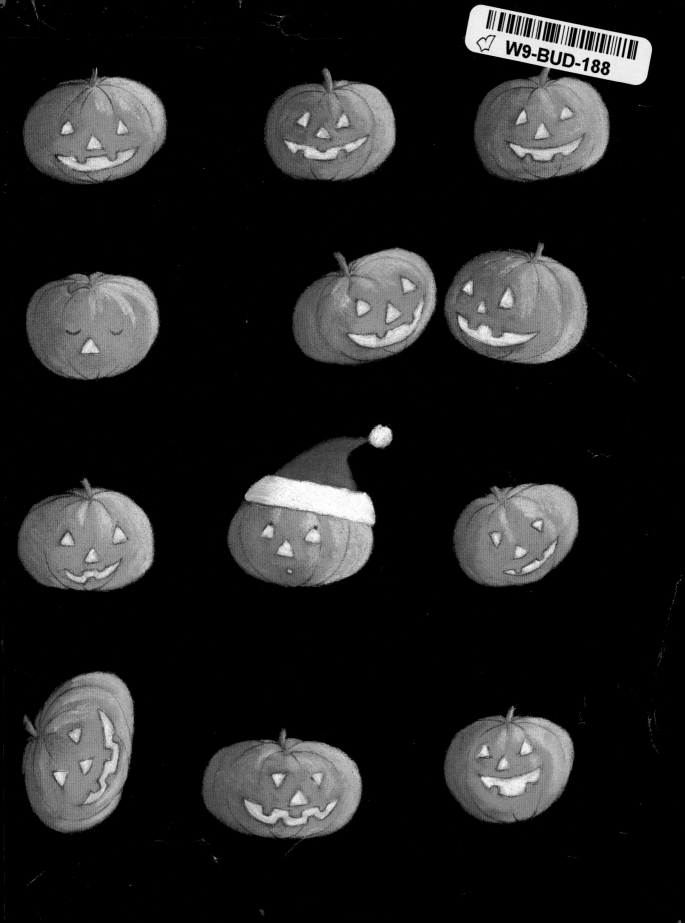

Merci à Chris et à Kylie

Margaret K. McElderry Books
An imprint of Simon & Schuster Children's Publishing Division
1230 Avenue of the Americas, New York, New York 10020
Text and illustrations copyright © 1998 by Hachette Livre
U.S. translation copyright © 2003 by Margaret K. McElderry Books, an imprint of
Simon & Schuster Children's Publishing
Originally published in France in 1998 as *Dis-moi, qu'est-ce que c'est Halloween?*
Book design by Kristin Smith
The text for this book is set in Hadriano.
The illustrations for this book are rendered in pastel.
Manufactured in China
2 4 6 8 10 9 7 5 3 1
Library of Congress Cataloging-in-Publication Data
Desmoinaux, Christel.
Hallo-what? / Christel Desmoinaux.— 1st ed.
p. cm.
Summary: A young witch wonders why everyone is so busy with pumpkins until her
grandmother tells her about Halloween and some of the traditions associated with it.
ISBN 0-689-84795-5 (hardcover)
[1. Halloween—Fiction. 2. Witches—Fiction.] I. Title.
PZ7.D4509 Hal 2003
[E]—dc21
2002151131

"Hallo-what?"

CHRISTEL DESMOINAUX

Margaret K. McElderry Books

New York • London • Toronto • Sydney • Singapore

One beautiful autumn day
the little witch Marceline was taking a
walk. Along the way she saw Petronille.
"Yoo-hoo! Petronille!" called Marceline.
"Where are you going in such a hurry?"

But she didn't hear the little witch.
Marceline decided to follow Petronille,
so she ran after her.

At the top of the hill Marceline found
Petronille and all the other witches
gathering pumpkins.

"What are you doing?" asked Marceline.

But the witches were far too busy to
pay attention to the little witch.

"What's happened to everyone?" Marceline asked herself. "It's as if I didn't exist!"

Then the little witch had an idea. "I'll visit Grandma. She'll know what's going on."

And off she ran to her grandmother's house.

Oh, no! Even Grandma was busy
with a pumpkin!

Marceline started to cry.

Grandma put the pumpkin down
and pulled Marceline onto her lap.

"Today is Halloween, little one,"
said Grandma.

"Hallo-*what*?" asked Marceline.

"Halloween," said Grandma.
"Now, dry your eyes and I'll tell
you all about it."

"For many years Halloween has been thought of as the scariest night of the year. Some people think it's the night when evil spirits come out."

Marceline shivered. "That's scary."

"It's supposed to be scary on Halloween," explained Grandma. "To protect themselves from evil spirits and witches flying around, people used to light huge bonfires."

"So Halloween is a witches' celebration?" asked Marceline.

"Exactly," said Grandma, "along with goblins, monsters, and everything else that's scary."

"But what about the pumpkins?" asked the little witch.

"According to Irish legend there once lived an old man named Jack. He was so stingy and mean that when he died he wasn't allowed to go to Heaven. But the Devil didn't want him either, so the Devil gave Jack a burning-hot cinder and sent him away. Jack put the glowing ember in a hollowed-out turnip to light his path. It's said that Jack is still wandering around with his lantern, looking for somewhere to rest."

"I still don't understand about the pumpkins,"
Marceline said.

"Well," said Grandma, "children make their
own lanterns to celebrate Halloween.
They're just like Jack's, except they use
pumpkins instead of turnips and they're called
jack-o'-lanterns. You see?"

"Yes!" Marceline clapped her hands.
"All these pumpkins will be
made into lanterns tonight!"

"Halloween has turned into a celebration mostly for children," said Grandma. "Long ago people thought wearing a costume would stop them from being seen by evil spirits. So now lots of children dress up like ghosts and vampires and even witches."

"That wouldn't be hard for me to do," the little witch said with a laugh.

"Then all the costumed children go from one neighbor's house to another saying 'Trick or Treat!' and people give them treats," Grandma explained.

"I want to wear a costume and get treats!"
Marceline cried, leaping off her grandmother's lap.
"I want Halloween!"

"All right," agreed Grandma. "Get your friends
and we'll have Halloween!"

Marceline found her best friends, Eglantine, Bobine, and Paraffine.

"Come with me to Grandma's house. We're going to have Halloween!"

"Hallo-*what*?" her friends asked.

"Grandma will tell you all about it," Marceline promised. "Grab a pumpkin and come on!"

Eglantine   Bobine   Paraffine

Soon four little witches with four large pumpkins were running as fast as they could go, all the way to Grandma's house.

"Come in, come in!" said Grandma.

Before long the four friends had carved their pumpkins . . .

and transformed themselves into a ghost,
a skeleton, a scary witch, and a vampire.
They were ready for trick-or-treating.

"Now," said Grandma, "for the
most important moment of all!" She
lit the candle in a pumpkin and put it in
the window. She gave the little witches
some bags and they went outside. The night
was aglow with orange jack-o'-lanterns.
"Stay together and good luck with your trick-or-
treating, little ones! I'll be watching you from the
window," said Grandma.
The little ghost, the little skeleton, the little witch, and
the little vampire ran next door to Petronille's house.

"Trick or treat!"

"You are all horribly horrible!" said Petronille, giving each an apple.

"Trick or treat!"

"Oh! You frightened me," said Gertrude, giving each a stick of candy.

"Trick or treat!"

"You are very spooky!" said Annabelle, giving each some popcorn.

"Trick or treat!"

"What scary costumes you have!" said Emily, giving each a cookie.

After they visited their neighbors,
the little ghost, the little skeleton,
the little witch, and the little
vampire were very tired and their
bags were very heavy. It was time
to go home.

At home Marceline took off her
costume, washed her face, and went
to bed. She put her bag of treats
right next to her bed so she'd see it
when she woke up in the morning.

Now I know what Halloween is, thought Marceline, *and I love it! I can't wait to have Halloween again next year!* And she fell asleep with the orange glow from the jack-o'-lanterns coming through her window.

Good night, Marceline, and happy Halloween!

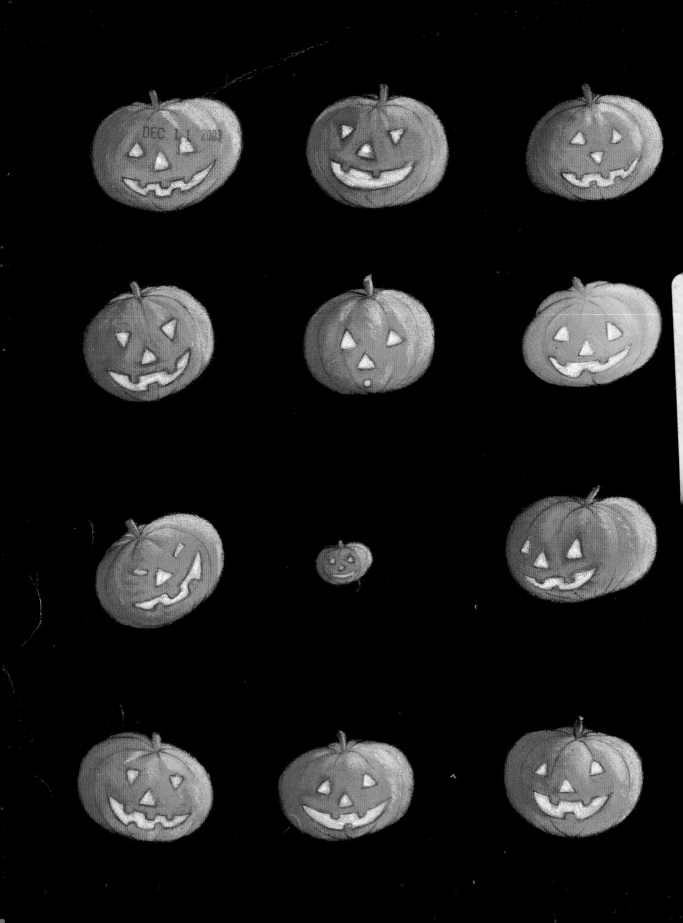